THE INTERGALACTIC KITCHEN SINKS

TAKE OFF WITH A KITE!

This lively series is designed for children who have developed reading fluency and enjoy reading complete books on their own.

The stories are attractively presented with plenty of illustrations which make them satisfying and fun! A perfect follow-on from the Read Alone series.

*By the same author*

RICKY ZEDEX AND THE SPOOKS

RICKY'S SUMMERTIME CHRISTMAS
    PRESENT

THE INTERGALACTIC KITCHEN

THE INTERGALACTIC KITCHEN GOES
    PREHISTORIC

FRANK RODGERS

# THE INTERGALACTIC KITCHEN SINKS

VIKING

VIKING

Published by the Penguin Group
Penguin Books Ltd, 27 Wrights Lane, London W8 5TZ, England
Penguin Books USA Inc., 375 Hudson Street, New York, New York 10014, USA
Penguin Books Australia Ltd, Ringwood, Victoria, Australia
Penguin Books Canada Ltd, 10 Alcorn Avenue, Toronto, Ontario, Canada M4V 3B2
Penguin Books (NZ) Ltd, 182–190 Wairau Road, Auckland 10, New Zealand

Penguin Books Ltd, Registered Offices: Harmondsworth, Middlesex, England

First published 1995
1 3 5 7 9 10 8 6 4 2

Made and printed in Great Britain by Butler & Tanner Ltd, Frome and London

A CIP catalogue record for this book is available from the British Library

ISBN 0–670–85376–3

Welcome to breakfast with the Birds.

Eventually everyone got organized and rushed out of the house. Mr Albert Bird and BB stayed at home. It was Albert's day off.

After everyone had gone, Mr Bird tidied the house and BB helped him to hang up the washing.

BB then went to feed Proto and Sarah, the two young Protoceratops dinosaurs that the family had brought back from their adventure in the prehistoric age.

BB had always wanted a horse and the dinosaurs were just the right size.

Startled, Mr Bird turned to see BB come riding round the corner of the house on Sarah.

Just at that moment, however, there was a terrific

Mr Bird jumped again, then sighed. The noise had come from BONCE (the National Bureau of Clever Experts) where he was janitor. They were always making a mess of experiments. There was no warning siren, so Albert knew it wasn't an emergency. He sighed again.

PROBABLY MEANS I'LL HAVE SOME CLEARING UP TO DO! AH, WELL.... AT LEAST THERE'S NO HARM DONE!

But Albert was wrong.

The sudden noise had startled Sarah and she went wild . . . kicking and rearing like a bucking bronco.

Mr Bird gasped as he saw what was happening.

But before Mr Bird could reach her, Sarah bolted . . . straight towards the kitchen.

She charged through the open door, then realizing that there was nowhere to go, she skidded to a halt.

BB shot over Sarah's head and sailed through the air. Luckily, she managed to grab hold of a box on the wall.

Unluckily, it was the box containing the START button for the kitchen's motor. BB hit it with a thump and heard a loud CLICK.

# RRRRR!!

The kitchen's motor burst into life.

BB climbed down to the floor, just as the protective screen sealed off the kitchen from the outside.

OH, OH, SARAH! I THINK WE'RE GOING TO GO FLYING!

DON'T PANIC, BB! I'LL THINK OF SOMETHING!

Mr Bird watched, horrified and helpless, as the kitchen trembled and slowly started to rise from the ground.

12

But it was too late. With a final RRRRR! the kitchen picked up speed and streaked into the sky.

Meanwhile, in the history class at school . . .

In the science class, Jay was conducting an experiment.

And in the gym, Robin had just climbed to the top of the wall-bars.

In the calm, quiet order of the library, Mrs Emily Bird was enjoying her work when . . .

As Snoo, Jay and Robin rushed out of the school gates, they met their mum running from the library and their dad sprinting from the house.

Mr Bird quickly explained what had happened.

Albert had a terrible memory. He knew that there was *something* that might affect the protective screen that went round the kitchen, but couldn't remember what it was.

Mr and Mrs Bird had built a new garden shed after the first one had been demolished in space. A new, improved version that could fly as well as the kitchen!

When they got back to the house, they found the
Clever Experts staring at the space where the kitchen
had been.

Mr Bird told them what had happened.

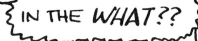

The family crammed into the shed and Mrs Bird pressed the START button.

The little building shuddered, wobbled a bit, then suddenly shot into the sky.

The Clever Experts hurried back to their laboratory at BONCE. Quickly and efficiently, they went about setting up a super-smart, long-range speech transmitter.

On the contrary . . . BB was enjoying the ride.

The kitchen streaked on . . .

. . . and on.

Meanwhile, back at BONCE, the Clever Experts were working like a well-oiled machine . . . a team . . . blending together unselfishly . . .

. . . when suddenly, one of them had an idea.

Quickly they connected a radio booster to the phone and dialled the kitchen's number. Everyone waited anxiously.

BB listened carefully. She set the wash programme to "spin", turned on the hot tap and switched on the light. That left one thing to do.

The kitchen shuddered to a halt above the ocean. Slowly it turned round, picked up speed and streaked for home.

The family saw this as they approached in the garden shed and cheered.

BB saw them and waved . . . then suddenly, she heard a strange noise coming from the shelf by the cooker.

She had no time to find out, because just then the
kitchen slowed down and stopped . . . hovering only a
few metres about the waves.

The family gasped in consternation.

But it wasn't all right, because just then . . .

Mr Bird suddenly gasped, snapped his fingers and grasped Emily by the arm.

The family watched, horrified, as the waves touched the bottom of the kitchen and then began to splash at the walls.

Mr Bird kicked off his shoes and opened the door of the shed.

But just as he was about to leap into the water, the kitchen door opened and out jumped Sarah . . .

... with BB on her back.

The little dinosaur swam powerfully away from the kitchen, which sank lower and lower and then disappeared from sight.

Mrs Bird brought the garden shed down until it was almost touching the waves.
 Sarah swam up to it.

BB was helped aboard first, then everyone helped to haul Sarah in. She was so heavy, however, that the shed began to sink too!

Mrs Bird pressed the BOOST button and the little shed shot upwards like a rocket. Quickly she got it under control and flew it homewards.

When they touched down, they found the Clever
Experts waiting for them.

DID YOU MANAGE TO TRACK THE KITCHEN AND SEE WHERE IT WENT?

WELL, YES... AND NO...

WE FOLLOWED IT AS IT SANK DEEPER AND DEEPER, THEN... IT JUST *VANISHED* FROM OUR SCREENS.

VANISHED?! NOW IT'S *REALLY* LOST!

MAYBE MR CRABBIT CAN HELP US FIND IT, DAD!

Mr Crabbit was the
government official
who had flight-
tested the kitchen.
Mr Bird gave him a
call but was
disappointed.

I'D LIKE TO HELP YOU, ALBERT... BUT THE GOVERNMENT DOESN'T THINK THAT THE INTERGALACTIC KITCHEN IS IMPORTANT ENOUGH TO RESCUE. NOW... IF IT WAS A NEW BOMBER OR A SPY SATELLITE...

Suddenly, one of the Clever Experts had a brainwave.

So the Clever Experts, helped by the family, set to work in the workshop at BONCE . . .

. . . and in no time at all, it was ready.

The garden shed was brought over and lifted inside.

Without wasting a moment, the whole family piled into the shed.

Mr Bird closed the doors and pressed the START button. The shed started to vibrate . . . the bubble-car did too . . . and gently the whole contraption lifted off the ground, gathered speed . . .

. . . and went soaring into the sky . . .

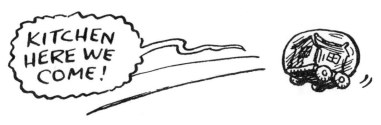

. . . where it levelled off and went streaking towards the ocean.

The garden shed sped on.

Suddenly, there was a ringing noise.

Mr Bird reached inside his pocket and took out a portable phone.

But it wasn't the Clever Experts at all.

Mr Bird didn't get a chance to explain because
Mr Krspltx went on . . .

I'M AFRAID THERE MIGHT BE A PROBLEM, KRL. OUR KITCHEN HAS SUNK IN THE OCEAN AND WE ARE ON OUR WAY TO FIND IT.

WHAT? OH, NO! THAT'S TERRIBLE FOR YOU... AND US! YOU SEE, THE PART WE LOST IS THE HOMING DEVICE FOR OUR SPACESHIP. WE WON'T BE ABLE TO GET HOME WITHOUT IT!

DON'T WORRY, KRL... WE'LL DO OUR BEST TO FIND THE KITCHEN.

GOOD LUCK! WE'LL COME AS FAST AS WE CAN TO HELP YOU. SPRKLFZ!*

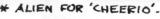

* ALIEN FOR 'CHEERIO'.

...ER... SPRKLFZ TO YOU TOO!

NOW WE REALLY MUST GET OUR KITCHEN BACK. ACTION STATIONS EVERYONE!

40

The family managed to get the garden shed to go even faster and soon it reached the exact spot where the kitchen had sunk.

Slowly, it was lowered towards the waves.

The shed sank deeper and deeper into the blackness.
Mr Bird switched on the lights and the family gasped.
Caught in the beam were two huge, menacing shapes.

The enormous fish didn't seem too pleased to see
them, because suddenly they charged . . . straight for
the shed.

Everyone held on to something as Dad pressed the acceleration button. The shed shot downwards, and the sharks flashed by overhead and disappeared into the darkness.

The family crowded round the windows and saw an amazing array of fish of all shapes and sizes as they sank into the depths.

Then, without warning, the shed abruptly stopped its downward movement and came to a standstill.

The little bubble-car-shed trundled around the sea-bed and the family stared anxiously out of the windows. After an hour, however, they had found nothing. Everyone was very disappointed. Their air supply was running low and they would have to go back to the surface. Just then an enormous circular shape appeared in front of them.

Jay consulted his book, *One Million Useful Facts.*

Good question . . . and the answer to it is . . .

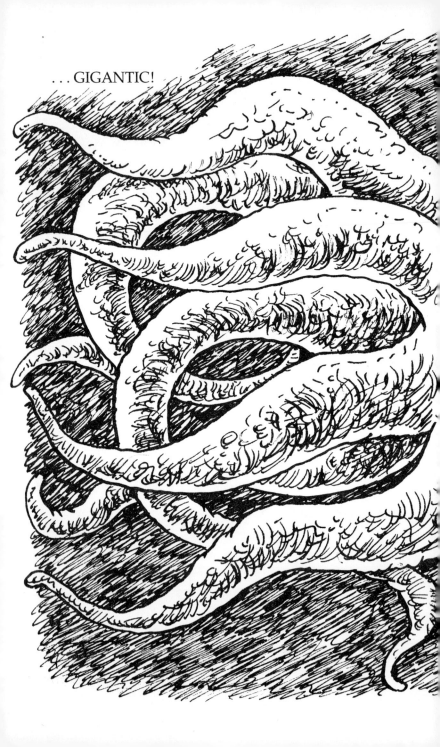

A sudden, violent lurch of the shed sent everyone sprawling against the walls.

Then BB, who was looking out of the back window, noticed something else.

Everyone turned to look out of BB's window and gasped.

The monster had stopped the squid in its tracks. Its huge mouth, full of teeth bigger than traffic-cones, opened slowly . . . the squid let go and swam away for dear life.

The monster edged nearer and nearer . . . but gradually the family realized that something strange was happening to it.

Nobody answered, because just at that moment
something else appeared . . .

. . . something else with three huge, bright eyes.

Correct! *Not* another monster. It was, in fact . . .

The Krspltxs' spaceship hovered above the bubble-car-shed and the Birds felt themselves being drawn upwards.

Seconds later they were inside.

Emily and the children had met Mrs Krspltx before, but Albert hadn't, so they were introduced.

＊ ALIEN FOR 'HELLO, NICE TO MEET YOU.'

Just then, BB heard a familiar sound . . . a sort of snuffling snort. She ran and opened a door.

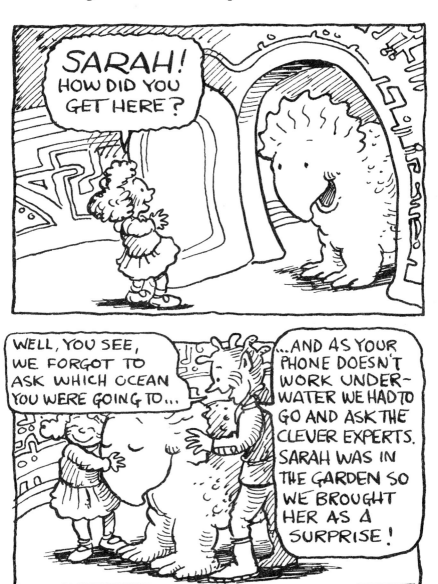

Mr and Mrs Krspltx manned their monitor screens and started to sweep the area for signs of the kitchen.

The Krspltxs' sophisticated scanner probed the depths for half an hour. At the end of it, the aliens shook their heads.

Everyone sat around feeling very depressed.

The Krspltxs had lost their homing device and the Birds had lost their kitchen.

CHEER UP, DAD. REMEMBER...WE'RE STILL ON HOLIDAY.

OF COURSE WE ARE, KRRSTY.

YES, I'M SURE SOMETHING WILL TURN UP, DEAR. IN THE MEANTIME, LET'S CARRY ON AS NORMAL.

GOOD IDEA..

WHY DON'T WE SHOW THE BIRDS ATLANTIS?

THE LOST CITY OF ATLANTIS? BUT THAT DOESN'T EXIST!

The spaceship slid through the dark water and soon arrived at a huge, black cave mouth.

Mr Krspltx pointed proudly.

Everyone gathered at the windows and peered into the dark tunnel. A light appeared up ahead. It grew bigger as they approached, until they saw it was a huge, neon sign which said . . .

The spaceship went through the entrance and followed an upward-pointing sign.

A moment later it broke the surface and emerged into a vast underground cavern.

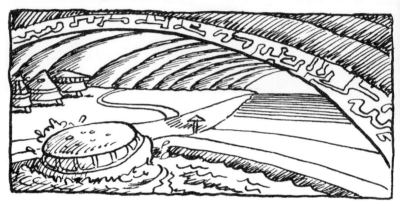

The first thing they saw was a sign which said . . . PLEASE LEAVE YOUR VEHICLE IN THE SPACESHIP PARK AND PROCEED ON FOOT.

So they parked at the end of a row of spaceships and everybody got out. BB even brought Sarah with her.

They were immediately met by a robot guide.

Mr Bird frowned. He didn't really like robots. He thought they were very unreliable things.

They were led to the top of a flight of stairs. When they got there they gasped. Atlantis, the lost city, the Intergalactic Fun Park, was stretched out before them.

They gazed in wonder at the incredible sight.
Suddenly, Snoo saw something that made her squeal
in excitement.

"Look everyone!" she cried. "It's . . ."

Everyone gasped. Sure enough, there it was . . .
nestling between a tower and a temple.

69

The robot guide was startled to see his party suddenly desert him and go rushing into the Fun Park.

When they got to the kitchen, however, there was a problem. Another robot!

Just then the robot's eyes lit on Sarah.

Mr Bird nodded his head. He thought it was worth a try. He whispered to BB and she agreed.

Everybody helped the robot to climb on to Sarah's back.

Sarah dutifully began to trot and the robot, a broad grin on his metal face, gave a wave.

The family watched as he rode up and down in front of the kitchen.

At that moment the cavern was lit up with a huge
FLASH, followed by . . .

It was obviously fireworks time at the Fun Park. The
children cheered, but the noise had frightened Sarah.

She began to rear and buck, the robot hanging on for
dear life . . .

. . . then she bolted . . . straight towards them.

Everyone dived to the side except BB. She ran into the
kitchen.

Sarah charged straight in after her. Once more she screeched to a halt and this time the robot went flying . . . right on to the START button.

The motor burst into life, the kitchen quivered and then shot straight upwards.

Mr Krspltx took charge.

THE KITCHEN WILL GO STRAIGHT OUT THROUGH THE TOP OF THE VOLCANO! COME ON... BACK TO THE SHIP!

Everyone raced back to the spaceship. It took off with a roar and streaked upwards in pursuit.

As they shot into the sunlight like a cork from a bottle, Robin spotted the kitchen.

THERE IT IS!

BUT IT'S GOING THE WRONG WAY!

Quickly Mrs Krspltx set up an electronic communicator and Mrs Bird spoke to BB.

The robot examined the motor and suddenly stuck his finger in a hole. There was a SZZZCH! sound and the kitchen, which was over New York by now, screeched to a halt.

The kitchen seemed to take a few moments to make up
its mind . . . then all of a sudden it dived down
towards the skyscrapers like a burst balloon . . .

before levelling out and streaking past the spaceship
on its way home.

79

Not long afterwards the kitchen landed at home and the spaceship touched down beside it.

The Clever Experts cheered when they saw the kitchen return safe and sound.

The family rushed out of the spaceship to meet BB.

Mr Bird had a slightly better opinion of robots now and thanked the metal cowboy for saving BB and the kitchen.

The Birds laid on a special party for the Krspltxes and the Clever Experts even baked a cake shaped like a sea monster. Everyone had a wonderful time.

But just as the party was finishing . . .

But they didn't. Everyone stared in surprise to see Proto and Sarah standing quite calmly beside CLNT YSTWD, the metal cowboy.

Just then, two of the "darned ol' Clever Experts" arrived from BONCE.

Suddenly, Mr Krspltx snapped his fingers.

YES...THANK YOU VERY MUCH, CLEVER EXPERTS... BECAUSE YOU HAVE REMINDED ME THAT I'VE GOT JUST WHAT THEY NEED!

He dashed into his spaceship and emerged a few moments later carrying a strange object.

JUST ATTACH THIS TO YOUR MOTOR AND THE KITCHEN WILL BE ABLE TO GO UNDERWATER.

WONDERFUL!

PERHAPS WE SHOULD TAKE CLEVER LESSONS FROM MR AND MRS KRSPLTX?

WHY DON'T WE TRY OUT THE UNDERWATER DEVICE, DAD?

YES...WE COULD TAKE THE KRSPLTXES TO ONE OF OUR FAVOURITE HOLIDAY PLACES.

SOUNDS LIKE A GOOD IDEA!

TERRIFIC! LET'S DO IT... *NOW!*

So . . . an hour later, the kitchen flew out of the clouds and dropped towards Loch Ness.

"Now you can meet one of *our* monsters, Krl," chuckled Mr Bird.

Mr Bird took this information rather well in the circumstances. Perhaps he was getting used to robots because he just sighed and grinned.